SPARE A THOUGHT AT CHRISTMAS

Edited by

Kelly Deacon

First published in Great Britain in 2000 by
TRIUMPH HOUSE
Remus House,
Coltsfoot Drive,
Woodston,
Peterborough, PE2 9JX
Telephone (01733) 898102

All Rights Reserved

Copyright Contributors 2000

HB ISBN 1 86161 731 3
SB ISBN 1 86161 736 4

FOREWORD

Spare A Thought At Christmas

Each Christmas while many of us are cherishing the love of friends and family we should also take time out to spare a thought for those who may be in need. There are many people who are unable to have a happy Christmas and whilst many of us are partying they are far from our minds.

The poems within this book help draw attention to those who are often neglected throughout the Christmas season whilst helping us to remember those who are less fortunate. By sharing a little of their own festive spirit and offering prayers of comfort to others, the authors of this book have made sure that those in need are not forgotten.

The result is a heart warming and compelling read that teaches us to be thankful while still remembering the real meaning of Christmas.

Kelly Deacon
Editor

CONTENTS

Homo Sapiens	B J Bramwell	1
Christmas Eve	Malcolm F Andrews	2
For Those Who Go Without	Dave Mountjoy	3
Tramp	Mary Rodwell	4
Wherever You May Go	Barbara Manning	5
Scrooge	Eunice Neale	6
Think Of Me At Christmas	Don Woods	7
Christmas Gifts	M G Bradshaw	8
Rejoice Only In Him!	Linda Afolabi	9
Christmas As Seen Through The Eyes Of A Child	Margaret Jenks	10
The Spirit Of Christmas	D W Hill	11
Adventures With Santa Claus	Jean P McGovern	12
The Meaning Of Christmas	Elizabeth Hawkins	14
Before Christmas	Anna Virkerman	15
The Loving Family	Don Goodwin	16
Christmas Spirit	Charlotte Biggs	17
Getting The Presents	Michael Hertz	18
Christmas Time	Lisa Candy	19
Piety	John P Evans	20
Nowell	Roberta Roberts	21
Christmas Time	Sharlotte Knox	22
Santa's Sleigh	Samuel Coveney	23
Christmas Spirit	Melissa Baigent	24
Christmas Time	Hayley Thompson	25
Christmas Time	Lauren Johnson	26
Christmas Time	Jason Waddilove	27
Father Christmas	Dean Bryant	28
Christmas Is Not About Presents	Kirsty Fuggle	29
Spirit Of Christmas	Kerry Martin	30
Christmas Eve	Alison Jackson	31
From Heaven With Love	Rosemary Ann Betts	32
Christmas	John Horton	33
A Christmas Cacophony	Anne Filkin	34
I Like	Jean Paisley	35

You Know Who Your Friends Are	J C Crowe	36
The Christmas Gift Of Life	Colin A Rixen	37
From Manger To Millennium	Lily May	38
The Spirit Of Christmas	J M Stoles	39
Christmas Air	Michaela Philp	40
Happy Day	Mary Fleming	41
The World's Children	Christine Mason	42
The Cries On Christmas Morning!	A Ogden	43
Xmas Gift	Lilian Young	44
Lucky Me	Bav	45
The Spirit Of Christmas	David J Hall	46
Star Child	Leigh Smith	47
Christmas	Joy Sharp	48
Christmas Joy	Peggy Chapman	49
A Time For Jesus	Colum Donnelly	50
Christmas Joy	P M Peet	51
Christmas	T A Saunders	52
Peace On Earth	Mary Lister	53
Christ Is Born	John M Beazley	54
Christmas Without You	Amanda Steel	55
Love Wish	Geof Farrar	56
Remember Christmas	Sara Newby	57
Moatfarm Infants' Nativity	Ann Hathaway	58
Christmas Is Coming	Kenneth Mood	59
Santa Came!	Margaret McHugh	61
Christmas Time!	Bianca Fairless	62
A Baby Has Been Born	Amanda-Jane Tudor	63
Christingle	Mavis Scarles	64
Christmas Memories	Lesley Stockley	65
The Gift Of Life	P W Sansom	66
Wiser Or Older	Terry Daley	67
Happy Christmas . . .	Flora Passant	68
Christmas Past	Judy Studd	69
Christmas In The Country	Marion Schoeberlein	70
I Remember Christmas	Joyce A W Edwards-Arnold	71
Shine A Light	Linda Storer Smith	72

Jesus, The Gift Of God	Muriel H Beck	73
You Were The One Love That Would Last: . . .	John Docherty	74
Christmas Eve	Denyce Alexander	76
Believe	Graham Jenkins	77
Christmas Rose	Andy Rosser	78
Christmas Greet	Howard Young	79
The True Message Of Christmas	Jane Marshall	80
Christmas Box	Kate Kerrigan	81
Christmas	Trisha Moreton	82
A Christmas Wish	Jane Manning	83
Yuletide	L J Needs	84
What's Left After Christmas?	B M Howard	85
The Message	Bakewell Burt	86
Christmas Time 1999	Joan Taylor	87
Christmas	Carole Osselton	88
War Child	Wayne Cregan	89
Nobody Cares	Kevin J Hodge	90
Kosovo Child	Wally	91
A Time To Remember	G Silver	92
A Christmas Thought	Sharon Evans	93
The Hotel	Joan E Blissett	94
Celebrating Christmas	Di Bagshawe	95
Christmas Spirit?	Anne Brown	96
Winter Thoughts	Gwen Hartland	97
A Moral Millennium	Doug Thomas	98
Poppies Of Flanders' Fields	Phyllis Blue	99
War Years 1914 To 1918	Olive Peck	100
A Christmas Wish	Kathleen Mary Scatchard	101
Spare A Thought At Christmas	Janine Thomas	102
A Prayer	Marcus Tyler	103·
Give Us Hope	Valerie Deering	104
No One Cares	Joy Willoughby	105
Just A Glimmer	Margaret Davies	106
Christmas Love	Alice Zamanian	107
Spare A Thought	Pauline M Wardle	108
Jesus Hold My Hand	Don Woods	109
Spare A Thought	Kane Saunders	110

Just Spare A Thought	Arthur Pickles	111
A Child's Cry For Peace	Lynda Fordham	112
Spare A Thought	Gordon Bannister	113
Remember Them	Mary Ferguson	114
Spare Just One Minute	Tara Woods	115
Spare A Thought	Dean Hallett	116
What Harm Could It Do To Help A Poor Person?	Jemma Hall	117
Spare A Thought	Matthew Reeves	118
Think Of Others	Kayleigh Gosling	119
Spirit Of Christmas	Laura Carpenter	120
Spare A Thought	Jessica Twydall	121
Spare A Thought	Kayleigh Stannage	122
Spare A Thought	Gina Curtis	123
Spare A Thought	Alex Payne	124
Christmas	Brenda Radford	125

HOMO SAPIENS

My family is the human race
and we are far apart
yet everyone I've met and know
lives daily in my heart

For each and every single one
is precious in my love
each child so different, so unique
each special in their way

For each I'd gladly write a verse
if I could pen the truth
but love expressed is shy
as my talent is with words

If I could write a poem
to each and every one
if I could tell them how I feel
the good that they have done

For love is life for everyone
the more we love we grow
and life is love for everyone
each person that we know

I cannot kill my brother
I cannot do him wrong
to harm him is to harm myself
and life is just too strong

Each race and nation have their faults
they have their virtues too
as each and every human soul
O God belongs to you.

B J Bramwell

CHRISTMAS EVE

Silently, as the world awaits His coming, I gaze upwards
through the nocturnal stillness to the Heavenly heights,
where twinkling stars lustrously glow
on this hallowed, frosty winter's night.
What mystery! What wonderment!
Will I see that guiding star which leads to Bethlehem
that drew travellers from afar?
Vainly I search, focusing only on infinity,
yet in my heart I know that He is there,
watching, waiting to be received.
Come Lord Jesus into this manifestly materialistic world;
Come, joyful and triumphant into the hearts of all your people,
rich and poor of every nation,
Come, let us celebrate your birth and rejoice!

Malcolm F Andrews

FOR THOSE WHO GO WITHOUT

Shopping, money, money, shops,
We search and search until we drops,
Is Christmas just a time to spend,
As if our pockets have no end.

So spare a thought this Christmas time
For those whose lives so rarely rhyme.
The down and outs who have no home,
No family warmth in which to roam.

And whilst we sit and stuff our faces
Think of all the different races
Who every day must all compete
For simply, just a bite to eat.

Of sympathy they have no need
Nor token gifts from the lands of greed,
Food is what they all require
To quench the thirst of a hungry fire.

You see, so many have so much
But really seem so out of touch
And as each Christmas comes and goes
The 'Call for more' just grows and grows.

And yet we all could lend a hand
To help the needy in each land
For after all, is it not true
That love lies in each one of you?

And love is such a special gift
Which gives each every heart a lift
That please, this Christmas, send some out
To those who always go without.

Dave Mountjoy

TRAMP

Tattered brown, like oily rags,
Filthy with age, tied with coarse string,
His ill-fitting, limp coat hangs,
While he scours the bins and pavements
For cigarette butts, odds and ends,
Cast offs, precious things to him.
And I wonder where and how he lives,
And why it is!

Mary Rodwell

Wherever You May Go

When you climb the highest mountain
You can know that God is there,
When you cross the barren desert
You can feel His presence near,
And if you are in danger
You can face the strongest foe,
For the love of God will be with you
Wherever you may go.

When you walk along the crowded street
You can know that God is there,
When you stop with strangers who you meet
You can feel His presence near,
And if at times you make mistakes
You can learn and you can grow,
For the love of God will be with you
Wherever you may go.

When you call to Him each morning
You can know that He is there,
When you listen for His answer
You can feel His presence near,
And if this world rejects you,
You can smile, because you know
That the love of God will be with you
Wherever you may go.

The love of God will be with you
Wherever you may go.

Barbara Manning

SCROOGE

How mean can a man be
so selfish he cannot see
the suffering he has caused
and it's only because
he wants more money
but it isn't very funny
when the wife is in pain
and they have to move again
to a bungalow with no steps
so they can stop all the frets
of falling down the bank
now let's be very frank
he took every penny
which never left them any
no money for a van
what a mean man.

Eunice Neale

THINK OF ME AT CHRISTMAS

In your joy on Christmas day
Think now and then of me
And place a gift, however small
Beneath your Christmas tree

A gift to show the world you care
For the stranger passing by
The poor drunkard or the homeless
That could be you or I

Misfortune can in seconds strike
So walk softly down life's road
Those you now scorn, soon you could join
And like them bear the load

A burden only can be eased
If someone that load will share
And all it takes is one kind word
To let a poor soul know you care

Don Woods

CHRISTMAS GIFTS

Christmas greetings to everyone,
These gifts we bring are new,
For they come from the spirit world,
We wish to give them to you.

Our first gift is of happiness,
To bring laughter to those in need,
To fill their hearts with gladness,
We plant a joyous seed.

Our second gift is for thoughts,
To send to those alone,
To those who have no family,
To those who have no home.

Our third gift is of understanding,
For those of different faiths,
To tolerate your fellow man,
No matter what colour or race.

Our fourth gift is of peace,
To place into the hearts of men,
To cease all the turmoil,
Never to war again.

Our final gift is from your loved ones,
Who have just come to say?
We wish you a Merry Christmas,
On this your special day.

M G Bradshaw

REJOICE ONLY IN HIM!

A mystical time,
There is enchantment in the air,
I am spellbound,
A surge to buy and to give has gripped me,
I rush to the shops, to buy a hamper,
The turkey in the window laments at its plight,
Rejoice I hear, there is free ale from the barrel,
Rejoice! Your credit has been increased,
Rejoice! A century has passed, passed into the past,
Then, my spirit halts me from my error,
'Rejoice not in ale,
Rejoice not in credit,
Rejoice not in time,
Rejoice only in Him,
The true Son of God,
Whose birth has saved you, from ale, credit and time!'

The lights fascinate me,
The shimmering tinsels are like diamonds from above,
The glistening balls adorn my tree,
The flowing fairy graces my treetop,
The climax in the saga makes my son yell,
'I am rejoicing,
Santa is coming!
Decked with my bike, ball and every good thing!'
Then again, my spirit speaks,
'Rejoice only in Him,
The true Son of God,
Only through His birth, are we provided, with every good thing!'

Linda Afolabi

CHRISTMAS AS SEEN THROUGH THE EYES OF A CHILD

Mummy is busy
So tells me to play
She does not want me
To get in her way

She is going to make a cake
The oven is hot
There's fruit on the table
And mincemeat in the pot

With all this cooking
Christmas must be near
I've sent a letter to 'Santa'
I hope he comes this year

I didn't ask for too much
That would not be fair
'Chocolates' for mum and
For dad, a bottle of 'beer'

Santa has so much to carry
So I'm not sure if he could
Bring a present as well for me -
Just a little dog puppy.

Margaret Jenks

THE SPIRIT OF CHRISTMAS

What is Christmas all about?
Carols are sung and children shout.
Where have we been for 2000 years?
What have we seen - some joy, many tears.
Pillage and war and death and destruction
Caused by man unto man, God's wayward creation.
Jesus is born in Bethlehem
And is visited by three wise men.
It is the birth of our Lord,
The renewal of the word
Which becomes flesh
Even in this millennium mesh
Of domes, wheels and regalia.
Will we turn the wheel of time into mania?
We'll be apt to remember
This December
The word and its meaning -
God, love, no demeaning
Of pleasure and joy
For grown-up and little one
Because Jesus the Son
Was once a small boy

D W Hill

ADVENTURES WITH SANTA CLAUS

Santa travels afar through the cold brisk snow
Jingling the bells with his jolly 'Oh ho'
He arrives with more adventures, but gets into scrapes
Maybe he will get there more quickly wearing ice skates

While he sings a jolly song, without a care or a worry
Although he is speeding, and is jolly well in a hurry
Skipping the traffic jams, as he goes the other way around
While the snow is jolly well settled, with ice on the ground

He falls from his sleigh, as the reindeers' heads prop on one side
Wondering what will happen next, as Santa slips on a slide
The service men come to the rescue and fixes the sledge
The reindeers are then frozen stiff, and seem to be on edge

The men hear a murmur of 'Oh no, oh ho' and a jolly oh, my
As they look around to see Santa Claus giving out that sigh
So, up he jolly rises, and safely back on the sleigh
While the reindeers thaw out, and the ice drips away

So, off they ride again on this jolly Christmas Eve
Just wondering if Santa has something else up his sleeve
Of course, the sleigh is supplied with gifts and toys
For good little girls and for good jolly boys

At last, Santa climbs down the chimney on this jolly cold night
I pray, please do not peep, because it may give him a fright
He has already had a few mishaps, while his journey was tough
And I feel quite sure, that he has had a jolly enough

I can jolly well picture Santa getting stuck down the chimney
But, please children, do not go out of your bedrooms to see
For the reindeers get impatient to go back to their land afar
Just sleep tight little children, and just wish upon the star

Dream on the good things, as Christmas morn draws near
Santa may have more adventures, with jolly good cheer, next year

Jean P McGovern

THE MEANING OF CHRISTMAS

Born in a stable, innocent babe,
Mother a virgin, free from all blame.
Sent by God's will, a nation to save,
Attacked and defenceless but lit by a flame.

To remember His birth is the reason we share
In festivities merry and thanks that He came,
But the price that He paid must not be forgot
As we worship together and praise in His name.

Jesus our Saviour, the light of the world,
Bless us and keep us in this coming year,
Bind us together in spirit and truth
And help us remember you always are near.

Elizabeth Hawkins

BEFORE CHRISTMAS

You open your eyes in the morning,
And see a new set outside.
Instead of the rain so boring,
To us came the brilliant light.

The ground is cover around,
The carpet is shining so fresh,
The air is clean and sound,
You see all is white in a flash.

Snowflakes are moving in a circle,
They perform an intricate dance.
It's amazing and looks like a miracle,
What big delight is in your glance.

You imagine for yourself the fir
And the twinkles that you'll light,
Your grandchildren's eyes so clear,
Their cheerful games so bright.

They are waiting for old Santa Claus
And his bag full of toys and sweets snacks.
Fuzzy moustache above his mouth,
His wide smile when he opens the sack.

You forget your age and your problems,
You are young, you are strong, full of life.
You are playing in all old games,
It's the happiest time - Christmas night.

Anna Virkerman

The Loving Family

I am so fortunate because I have got
A loving family and I'm content with my lot.
But there are those that Christmas will only bring
Christmas carols that no one will sing.
Coloured crackers with no one to pull them
The hours stretched that last forever.
Will the day ever end, she thinks never.
Alone on Christmas day and Christmas night,
Every sound you hear it gives you fright.
So remember those whose Christmas will not be
Spent with a loving, caring, concerning family.

Don Goodwin

CHRISTMAS SPIRIT

Christmas is a time of year
When everyone gets together
To celebrate the birth
Of Jesus in a manger.
Santa falling down the chimney
Landing with a thump,
The Christmas tree all sparkly
With the angel on the top.
But don't forget what
Christmas is really all about. .

Charlotte Biggs (9)

GETTING THE PRESENTS

Mums and dads are rushing around,
Presents falling to the ground.
I'm trying to get to mum and dad,
But they keep on saying -
'Wait my lad.'
I hope they're buying something for me,
To put beneath our Christmas tree.

Michael Hertz (9)

CHRISTMAS TIME

Christmas is coming
   - hooray, hooray.
But it's not Christmas yet,
   I have to wait.
I lie in my bed waiting
   for it to come.
I hear a rustling noise
   from down below,
Then a thump,
   I run down the stairs.
There he is all dusty and black,
He hasn't seen me - he looks
   for his sack,
As he turns around,
   what does he see?
The lovely mince pies left on the plate,
No wonder he's bigger than me!

Lisa Candy (9)

PIETY

Virgin white snow cloaks the ground,
Yuletide greetings are cast abound.
Evergreen trees fashion holly,
While nature's feathered friends on bird tables folly.
Trees alight at Christmas time,
With tuneful voice singing festive rhyme.
Angelic hosts act out a nativity play,
Presents adorning trees, awaiting Christmas day.
Seasonal cards encompassed by biblical leaf,
The 25th of December, mirrors our religious belief.

John P Evans

Nowell

Christmas - time of joy and mirth,
Goodwill to all and peace on earth.
But let me tell you this, machree,
These sentiments come late to me.

Christmas cards in August see;
September, trimmings for the tree.
Adverts on the television -
Its punishment without remission.

We send cards and presents with jolly cheers
To folk who've not bothered with us in years.
And have you noticed, though you send a stack,
How many folk don't send one back?

Now it seems like envy, greed,
Folk spending far more than they need.
Gluttony, meat and poultry carving
While half the world is poor and starving.

If, in the East, a star shone bright,
You wouldn't see it for the neon light.
And if He spoke from the surrounding hills
He'd not be heard for jingling tills.

I think we tend to forget the reason
For this wondrous winter season.
We rush around looking cross and grim,
And seldom give a thought to Him.

But when the blessed day has dawned,
And I have risen, dressed and yawned.
I know how great is He who brought
Forgiveness for each un-Christian thought.

Roberta Roberts

CHRISTMAS TIME

Christmas, Christmas,
I love
Christmas,
And especially all the holly
Which grows on the green bushes,
And the angel on top of the
Bright Christmas tree,
And Christmas time is the time
When I wish everybody could be happy.

Sharlotte Knox (10)

SANTA'S SLEIGH

Santa's sleigh is full of toys
Waiting for the girls and boys,
And it seems to be getting
Heavier every year!
With reindeer at the front,
Without a snort or grunt,
They plunge Santa's sleigh into the air!
When it lands on the roof,
You can hear Rudolf's hoof.
But when they take off again
What a noise!
So jump up on his sleigh
And you'll be well on your way,
For another Merry Christmas!

Samuel Coveney (10)

CHRISTMAS SPIRIT

It's time for Christmas,
It's time for fun,
It's time to be good for mum,
I'm looking in my stocking,
I'm looking round the door,
My mum sees me and shouts
'Back to bed!'
I stamp my foot on the floor!

Melissa Baigent (10)

CHRISTMAS TIME

Now is Christmas time,
Ring a bell and sing a rhyme.
Santa will come at night,
While the Christmas tree is alight.
Marvellous new presents just for me,
All put with care under the beautiful tree.
I think how lucky we all are,
My brother playing with his brand new car.
Soon another year has passed,
Maybe next time it will last.

Hayley Thompson (11)

CHRISTMAS TIME

Christmas time is happy,
Christmas time can be sad,
Christmas time is really nice,
Because I'm really glad.

I love Christmas, I really do,
But one thing would make it right,
To wake up Christmas morning,
And find the ground all white.

Lauren Johnson (9)

CHRISTMAS TIME

Christmas time,
It's time for fun,
Meet friends and family and everyone.

Christmas time,
It's time for fun,
Eat Christmas dinner,
Yum! Yum! Yum!

Jason Waddilove (10)

FATHER CHRISTMAS

Poor Father Christmas rushing around,
In his sleigh going up and down,
With Rudolf and his nose shining bright,
He'd rather be where you are - in bed at night,
Delivering presents in the pale star light,
Leaving mince pies out, he might take a bite,
Elves are getting the presents ready,
Some are looking after reindeer 'Steady girl, steady!'
Come the morning children are happy, none sad,
Everyone smiling, even my dad.

Dean Bryant (10)

CHRISTMAS IS NOT ABOUT PRESENTS

Christmas is not about presents,
It's Jesus' birthday you know,
It's time for family and friends,
Not just Santa 'Ho, ho, ho.'
Christmas is not about food,
You should be thinking now,
It's not just about yourself you know,
It's Jesus' birthday 'Wow!'

Kirsty Fuggle (10)

SPIRIT OF CHRISTMAS

It's not the Christmas spirit
that roams around your empty hall,
and slithers through the brick dusty wall.
It's not the ghost that's filled with horror,
it's the one who brings fun.
So the Christmas spirit brings people joy,
remember Christmas is not just about
your favourite toy.

Kerry Martin (9)

CHRISTMAS EVE

As trees go up and lights are switched on,
People are dashing round town,
Money is spent on last minute food,
Santa's on his way, finding chimneys to climb down.

Although there is fog and frost is on the ground
We are still happy and all of good cheer,
For in a few hours, we will celebrate
The birth of the baby, our saviour so dear.

Presents are put round the decorated tree,
Mistletoe and tinsel, hang under the lights,
Children are sleeping, their stockings are filled
Outside it is dark, but within all is bright.

The snow falls on this cold and frosty night,
Around the crib everyone is singing,
Midnight arrives, *Merry Christmas,* is the greeting,
In town and in villages the bells are ringing.

Alison Jackson

FROM HEAVEN WITH LOVE

Hello angel, up there on the tree
I see you, looking down on me,
With your smiling face
And twinkly eyes,
The colour of the summer skies,
Floaty dress and dainty wings,
You look so lovely, my heart sings.

What a lovely angel!
Such a sight to see,
Standing guard high up there
On the Christmas tree.
Minding all the little lights,
The baubles and the tinsel,
Presents at the bottom
And the stockings on the lintel.

Were you with the brightest star
That led the donkey from afar,
To the stable where Jesus was born
On that first holy Christmas morn
And guard that Holy Family
As you now do our Christmas Tree
To remind us that from Heaven above
God sent His greatest gift 'with love'.

Rosemary Ann Betts

CHRISTMAS

While stars peep
The world's asleep,
All is still.
Shepherds watch,
Angels shine,
Light on the hill.
Mary and Joseph
In stable warm,
Quietly wait
Christ to be born.
Ox and ass
Shelter from storm,
Give up their bed,
For Christ to be born.
A star shines,
Magi bring,
Gifts for a king,
Gold for a crown,
Incense for God,
Myrrh for a grave,
Angels sing,
Bells ring,
Come the dawn
Christmas morn,
Rejoice,
Christ is born.

John Horton

A Christmas Cacophony

    At this dull season of the year
    Christmas carollers bring good cheer.
    But as to the reason why they're here -
    Those who *listen* are those who *hear.*

Hark! the herald angels sing
Glory to the new born king . . .
    Can't you turn that radio down,
    I can't hear a blessed thing!

Good King Wenceslas looked out
On the Feast of Stephen
When the snow lay round about . . .
    Who on earth was Stephen?

Glory to God in the highest, and to the earth be peace . . .
    That reminds me, get a turkey
    Goose is full of grease.

Here we come-a-wassailing! . . . a-rollicking, a-roistering,
    But in a silence, if we will,
    We can hear the angels still.
    To feel a *mystery*, that's the test . . .
    God may well smile at all the rest.

Anne Filkin

I Like

I like a dark cathedral just
candles in the dim,
a lovely crib where you can pray
and feel closer to him.

I like my Christmas dinner when
it's on the table spread,
it's strange though how it makes
you think of others who are dead.

I like Kings College Carols after
I have cooked the bird,
a few glasses of Archers after
children's songs are heard.

I like to watch the Passion Play
at my granddaughter's school,
to let go of such history you'd
have to be a fool.

Jean Paisley

YOU KNOW WHO YOUR FRIENDS ARE

You know who your friends are
They are always there
In foul weather -
And fair
You know who your friends are.

You know who your friends are
When your troubles are known
They're at the end of the phone
You know who your friends are.

You know who your friends are
They give till it hurts
Not in spasms and spurts
You know who your friends are.

You know who your friends are
They give unconditional love
Sent from above
You know who your friends are.

You know who your friends are
No matter how life's road will wend
They're still there at the end
You know who your friends are.

J C Crowe

THE CHRISTMAS GIFT OF LIFE

Christmas will come and Christmas will go
Some black, some grey and some with huge falls of snow
Pressed against the window, the children's faces glow
Excited eyes watch the skies and eagerly anticipate the sight
of a falling flake
A log burns and crackles in the fiery grate
Its warmth cuddling the watchers as they ensure that Santa won't be late

The world view of Christmas is materialism
Everyone concerned with what they've bought for so and so
Dashing, rushing about making sure they forget no one
Yet, ironically they overlook Jesus
Who gave the greatest gift of all.

There was no snow for him or room at the inn
When Joseph asked 2000 years ago
With Mary far from thin!
In a stable, with a donkey, straw and flies for company
She bore the son of man - our Saviour
Whose journey - our salvation, had only just begun.

It's Christmas in our world of plenty and it's good to be alive
Oh yes, forget the planning and the stress - leave that at the
foot of the cross
Jesus and God know best.

Spare a thought for those on earth who haven't such assurance
For whom the church bells that ring out are the clanging
chimes of doom
And thank God that, but for his grace that person, that situation
Could so easily have been you.

Gift wrapped presents, hearty convivial meals are fine
But don't let the truth get smothered in the mists of time.

Colin A Rixen

FROM MANGER TO MILLENNIUM

It is indeed a miracle we have come this far,
From manger to millennium by the brightest star.
Shepherds and kings knelt in the hay,
To pay homage to Jesus our king, that day.
What a wonderful time in history for all mankind,
Goodness has prevailed, let's keep this in mind.

The children in need, we must love and feed,
Take care of the sick and lowly.
Remember always when Jesus was born,
Always keep it holy.
He brought us through these troubled years
To this millennium new!

Sing out, rejoice 2000 years have passed,
The Lord's 'new world' for you!

Lily May

THE SPIRIT OF CHRISTMAS

A thatched cottage with pink roses
Around the door
17th century home
With ingle nooks and wood burning fire
And lots of Christmas decorations
Welcome you.
Snaky garden path, round a corner
And you are met with a snow-white snowman
With his warm smile to greet you
Orchard trees and bumblebees and
Herb garden, surround tall green
Christmas trees.
My magic cottage is hidden in a wooden scenic area
Cataclysmic views panel parallel lines
And a Santa hides just behind a heavy fir tree.
Magic and mystic aura's hover
And a black cat haunts restless shadows on a
Cold, crisp Christmas morning.

J M Stoles

CHRISTMAS AIR

All in the green leaf lies a flame
Calls a maiden by her name.
Bring a lily from the field,
A gift of love.

All in the bright sky gleams a star,
Hails a boy child from afar.
Bring a golden spark, a frost,
A gift of light.

All on the holly, berries shine,
Candles glow, their four lights shine.
Bring a carol, dancing round
A gift of joy.

All Christian folk now sing the tree,
The green wood cross that sets us free.
Bring a heart, a broken heart,
A gift of pain.

Flower, star, the maiden fine,
Save mankind and conquer time.
Sing the babe, the Holy Child,
A gift divine.

Michaela Philp

HAPPY DAY

Merrily the bells are ringing,
In the churches choirs are singing,
Round the world prayers are winging,
Love and peace to all men bringing
on this joyful Christmas morning.

The Sunday School children in colourful array
perform for us their nativity play,
Its message as meaningful today
as it was two distant millennia away
on that first Christmas morning.

Around the Holy Child there stands
kings and wise men from foreign lands
and humble shepherds led by a star
come to worship from afar
on the first Christmas morning.

Mary and Joseph look tenderly on
as gifts are laid at the feet of their son.
What wealth to grace a humble stall!
but love is the greatest gift of all
to bless the Christmas morning.

So serious the children, as each plays their part
the words and actions come straight from the heart.
'Away in a manger', their sweet voices sing
and this . . . the true Spirit of Christmas they bring
on this special Christmas morning.

Mary Fleming

THE WORLD'S CHILDREN

Children in their innocence are such a joy and pleasure
And if you love them they in turn will give it back forever
Many children don't know how 'cause love's been denied them
Through bitter conflict and famine
They're starved of mere affection
Adults of the world unite and give them your protection
Stretch out a hand readily, see the hope it brings
Let them succour greedily
May they feast like kings
Offer them the knowledge that they so clearly crave
Honour them with friendship they deserve for being brave
Children are the same the whole world over
They laugh and cry and hunger too
They need the love of me and you
Let's love our children, do it now
Make it a goal, make it a vow.

Christine Mason

THE CRIES ON CHRISTMAS MORNING!

Oh, the suspense on the night before Christmas!
Ah, the excitement and joy!
Children's eyes wide with the wonder of waiting,
Each pink girl and blue hopeful boy.

Young hearts a-flutter at the coming time -
Soon eyelids go heavy with sleep.
Could it be? Can it be? Hope it is just that
One night there's no need to count sheep!

Strangely shaped boxes and parcels and wrappings,
Xmas tree gleaming with bright sparkling light!
Branches all loaded and glittering with tinsel,
Just for this one special all-children's night!

What of the big day that comes in the morning?
Small feet rush down to examine the hoard.
Cries of delight and great whoops of laughter
Of now fulfilled
   Youthful excitement
      Long stored!

A Ogden

Xmas Gift

Christmas time was special
    Playing in the snow
Rosy cheeks all aglow.

    Sitting by the fireside
On a cold winter's night
    Sometimes a candle lit
Was our only light.

    We would toast our bread
One slice a head.

    We'd sit and talk and yap for hours
My mam would show us
    And make paper flowers.

Out came the frame dad would put it up
    Sitting at the table
Ginger wine we'd sup.

    A clippy mat was for all to see
We all had a go after our tea.

    The girls had a rag doll
Brother got a train
    Yes, our Xmas was special
I'm glad Santa came.

Lilian Young

LUCKY ME

Let's celebrate
it's Christmas

At a time of joy
and new birth

Meeting friends
and opening gifts

Take a moment
and think

How lucky we
exist.

Bav

THE SPIRIT OF CHRISTMAS

Don't forget this Christmas
That upon Christmas day
Jesus Christ was born
When you're celebrating your Christmas
Guide a thought to Jesus Christ

The true spirit of Christmas
Jesus Christ I believe would be glad
We all enjoy ourselves on His birthday
The act of giving a present to friends and loved ones

The spirit of Christmas
In your prayers give a thought for Jesus Christ
Born upon Christmas day, 25th of December
In Bethlehem

Enjoy your Christmas, enjoy your presents
Enjoy your friends, enjoy your loved ones
But go give a thought to the spirit of Christmas
That is on Christmas day, 25th of December
That Jesus Christ was born

Do remember and spare a thought in your prayers
This Christmas and others
Do keep a thought throughout the year
Jesus Christ loves us all

David J Hall

STAR CHILD
(For a new millennium)

Far in the western sky a lone star glows,
The long day draws to a weary, footsore close -
    But there is no room at the inn . . .
A stable-cave hewn from the rock -
Cold shelter for these weary travellers;
The silent cattle's steaming breath
The only sign of warmth -
    But there is dry straw on the earthen floor;
    There Mary rests, while Joseph watches -
    She is very near her time . . .

And then . . .
    That distant star -
    A point of light in the dark sky -
    Soars into the deepening blue,
    A shining arc of angel-light
    Rising and growing and brightening
    High above the night-bound earth
    Until, with the cry of a child,
    It bursts upon the darkened world
     In a blaze of shimmering glory -

        And Christ is born . . .

        *

And through two thousand years
His Life, His Sacrifice,
Has been our guiding star -
And still He bids us follow . . .
    Take His hand and go with Him
    Through the starlit years to come . . .

Leigh Smith

CHRISTMAS

Christmas bells a-chiming
Holly leaves a-shining
All go to make a Christmas
Happy and bright

A bright star above
Showering us with God's love
The star shines above the stable
Where the dear Lord Jesus lays

Hearts a-praying
Donkeys a-braying
As sweet praises we sing
To the dear Lord Jesus

Let Jesus live in your heart
Let your sin depart
Celebrate the birth of the Holy one
God's miraculous chosen Son.

Joy Sharp

CHRISTMAS JOY

There's a kind of hush in December, as the year rolls gently by,
A quietness in the mornings and, a greyness in the sky.
As nature's colours begin to fade, dark shadows now fill the night,
The earth is preparing for its rest, to make another springtime bright.

But another wonder awaits us, in this changing world we find,
The love and hope of Christmas, and an enduring peace of mind.
For when the Holy Christ-child, came to live upon this earth,
December means we celebrate, His holy wondrous birth.

And the joy of that first Christmas links our families and friends,
Giving us hope toward the future, with God's love that knows no end.
So grant us the understanding Lord, give us peace in word and mind,
May this Christmas bring us joyfulness, in Your promise to mankind.

For Christmas with its special message and the comfort that it brings,
Is the power and the glory, thank you Lord for all these things.

Peggy Chapman

A Time For Jesus

A little baby was crying,
wrapped in swaddling clothes,
he had his mother beside him,
comfortable from winter snows.

To all at home at Christmas,
everything is bright with joy.
Gifts remind us all of Jesus, with wise
travellers, from the course of the starry sky.

Christmas trees with lights, are
found on streets, in town and city.
They are also in the house at home,
with tinsel and decorations, colourful and pretty.

Santa Claus, meets the children in
the community, with a red garment and big white beard.
He has a stack of parcels, lovely gifts to give,
and sheds joy to the heart, his mystic story heard.

The story of Jesus is celebrated,
in churches across the land.
With love and fidelity, his memory is atmospheric;
with friends and relations, lovely hours pass by,
in waiting of times beyond.

The food we eat at Christmas,
is that of a king,
the turkey and the plum pudding,
make a great feast, with stockings the family bring.

Christmas carols make the spirit of
this time, really nice and true.
Social life is great and merry
the form of the crowd, expressed with the family few.

Colum Donnelly

CHRISTMAS JOY

Church bells will herald in the dawn
Reminding all it's Christmas morn
Their message of goodwill and peace
Those joyful words that never cease

Long years ago in Bethlehem
No room at all inside an inn
So in a stable dark and dim
Life of dear Jesus did begin

Stars shone brightly overhead
All glory beamed around that shed
A babe so very meek and mild
Proved to be the Holy Child

In peace and all tranquillity
This child grew our Lord to be
Who gave great love the world to know
Before He died for us below.

P M Peet

CHRISTMAS

At this time of year
People should be happy
And give good cheer
The holly, the ivy and the mistletoe
People taking their time . . .
Going slow.
Enjoying good food and wine
Believing in God and following the sign.
This is what Christmas is about
Giving to others and loving
God's word . . . shout.

Think of those not as fortunate as you
Without a loving family . . . not having what we've got
And may be without believing too.
A thoughtful moment to reflect
On the past year's achievements
And the odd regret.
The Christmas atmosphere
So great . . . it should always be here.
Decorations and everything
And church where we all sing.
The Christmas story being told
Jesus being born in Bethlehem
In a stable . . . so cold.

God be with you for evermore
Let him show you the way
Don't shut the door.

T A Saunders

PEACE ON EARTH

There is such quiet tranquillity
As we remember Jesus' nativity,
At Christmas, especially Christmas Eve,
A special peace surrounds the earth
To celebrate, as we believe,
Our blessed Saviour's birth.
People are friendly, wishing all well,
Children are happy and thrilled.
Everyone, old or young, fall under the spell.
As the noise and bustle are stilled.
We remember our loved ones and those we have lost,
Somehow they're nearer just now
They were saved by sweet Jesus, our Saviour, at cost.
So thank Him, as our heads we bow.

Mary Lister

CHRIST IS BORN

Sweet infant Holy, sweet infant lowly,
Bright star of morning brings the dawn,
Bells merrily ringing, choirs gaily singing, glad tidings bringing,
Christ is born!

Sleep gently holds Him, beauty enfolds Him,
Loving arms cradle, free from harm,
Bells merrily ringing, choirs gaily singing, glad tidings bringing,
Christ is born!

Soon comes the morrow, laden with sorrow,
Soon comes the heart ache, darkness and scorn.
Soon comes the smiter, piercing and bitter,
Soon comes the nail, the crown of cruel thorn.

Shepherds adore Him, bow down before Him,
Angels in heaven hail the morn,
Bells merrily ringing, choirs gaily singing, glad tidings bringing,
Christ is born!

John M Beazley

CHRISTMAS WITHOUT YOU

This year I'll eat and drink
Trying not to stop and think
Open all my presents and smile
I can only pretend for a while
Surrounded by family and friends
But it's you I really miss
I wish you were underneath this mistletoe with me
To share that special Christmas kiss
I try not to let others see
Without you here there's a hole in my heart
It can't be filled while we're apart
As much as I don't want you to be sad
Part of me hopes you feel the same way too
You're the only true love I've ever had
Christmas won't be the same without you.

Amanda Steel

LOVE WISH

Prayer dost give you mental strength
Expounds the mind, for silent wealth
Accords the truth of silent prayer
Compose each life, with patient thought
Elucidate the love, by Jesus bought

Be each to one and one to all
Elated throng, where good bears all

Undo your wrong, make true amends
Nurse the sick, straight all wrong trends
Take care of those, who make amends
Opine of love, for all, each trends

Yearn for love of Jesus Christ
On all, for all, for Jesus Christ
Unite in peace, with Jesus Christ

Geof Farrar

REMEMBER CHRISTMAS

When you're dreaming,
roasting chestnuts on the fire.
When you've unwrapped all
the gifts of your desire.
When you have filled the
Christmas tree with decorations
take a precious moment - remember
why we have Christmas celebrations.
On that very first Christmas day,
God gave us his only Son.
He was born to bring peace and
love and hope to everyone.
Christmas is a happy time to
exchange presents - laugh and sing.
So let us raise our glasses now
and drink a toast to Christ - the King.

Sara Newby

Moatfarm Infants' Nativity

Little faces came to tell
Of Christmas carols they sang so well
With silver crowns upon each head
A message for Jesus each little one said
A Martian dressed in white so bold
Rejoiced in story the children told
Mary and Joseph came meek and mild
Seeking shelter to have their child
Three wise men just wee little boys
Came to bring Jesus presents and toys
King in gold came proud and splendid
And angels from heaven soon descended
Each little face a silvery moonbeam
All sweetly singing just like a dream

Ann Hathaway

CHRISTMAS IS COMING

Christmas is coming near,
Buying presents, getting on the Internet,
And sending out cards,
All my energy running away like melted snow.

So off I go into Christmas wonderland,
Filled with parties and good cheer,
Singing carols and watching coloured lights,
Talking to Dad in the Nursing Home,
Waiting for Santa Claus and God,
To sort me out and guide me through
Till the coming millennium year.

Kenneth Mood

SANTA CAME!

Christmas Eve, and times were hard,
How do you tell a child
That Santa would not be calling here?
They just looked up at you and smiled.

Toys were too expensive,
No money left to buy
Even the smallest plaything,
So parents had to try

To make and fashion toys themselves
Which always turned out well,
Out would come Dad's tool box
And Mum's sewing machine as well.

An old wooden box with the sides knocked out
Made a wagon, on which to ride,
Some old rope to steer it with
And two wheels on either side.

Next, Mum would cut up her old 'glad rags'
To make a teddy bear,
With embroidered eyes and nose and mouth,
For which she had a flair.

Any material left over,
She would turn into a doll,
Some strands of wool would make its hair,
A child's favourite toy - the old rag doll.

And on Christmas morn
When the children woke -
'We knew Santa would be sure to call'
Were the first words that they spoke.

And the parents smiled and looked on with pride
At Susie's doll and Jimmy's ride!

Margaret McHugh

CHRISTMAS TIME!

It's time once again for St Nicholas Day,
It's much much colder than April or May.
It's time to remember what this day means,
It's not just for receiving presents, or so it seems.
The colours of Christmas are red and gold,
But outside your home, it's windy and cold.
It's a time for kindness and joy,
For every little girl and boy,
Getting excited for Christmas Day,
When looking at gifts people forget what to say.
Turkey and stuffing, all that nice food,
.This all adds to the Christmas mood.
Let's all remember what Christmas is for,
And enjoy Christmas for evermore!

Bianca Fairless

A BABY HAS BEEN BORN

Looking back on the past
I can see the stars shining
Looking back on the past
I see stars in their eyes
For they knew of the birth
And of Jesus' coming
For they knew it would bring
Peace upon earth.
Trumpets sound, salute the happy morning,
Trumpets sound, a baby has been born.

Looking back on the past
I see shepherds in the stable
Looking back on the past
I see kings bowing low.
They bring gifts from afar
They are filled with awe and wonder
For their Saviour has been born
He will live for evermore.
Trumpets sound, salute the happy morning,
Trumpets sound, a baby has been born.

Looking back on the past
This baby is so precious
Looking back on the past
Where would we be now?
Look to the future
We can do something about it
Let's look in front us
As we have looked behind.
Trumpets sound, salute the happy morning
Trumpets sound, a baby has been born.

Amanda-Jane Tudor

CHRISTINGLE

Have you heard of 'Christingle'? It's the name
Of a special service once a year, held in our churches
Mainly aimed at children and their families there.
(A scent of oranges fills the air as we sit close for warmth
along the pew.) A reading is chosen to express
Suitable words for a special theme,
A theme of God's love in Christ His Son,
Who made His act of love supreme.

Into the children's hands are given (to symbolise the world)
An orange, encircled with a blood-red ribbon.
The ribbon is Jesus' sacrifice,
But rising above is a candle of white
With flickering, shining, living flame,
Unvanquished is the world's true light,
The light of Christ.
Always the same, constant and bright.

We sing our hymns and say a prayer remembering
Those less fortunate, victims of homelessness,
And war, of hunger, loss and mistreatment.
We think of the sorrow in this world and make our contributions now.
The plate is passed. We hope our gifts will help to heal, and nourish.
Maybe bring a hint of love at last to those whose hopes are fading fast.

But let us not so easily surrender
Our responsibility, as each of us lays down a
Gift of money on the plate.
For Christ laid down His life.
Let us all share, let us all give,
Let us love all God's world
Before it is too late.

Mavis Scarles

CHRISTMAS MEMORIES

Chestnuts sweet and roasting, our fingers yet to burn
Pulling Christmas crackers, impatient for our turn
Raking out my pillowcase to see what Santa gave
Little bits and pieces he knows I like to save
Aromas from the kitchen and smells of nutmeg spice
Pine tree dressed in winter garb and looking very nice
Holly branch with berries that's pinned above the door
Mistletoe just teasing fresh kisses to explore
Grandad dozing peacefully, his paper crown askew
Children all a-dither, not knowing what to do
Nana watching telly, she's waiting for the Queen
Our cat up on the table pinching pudding cream
Dad's now cracking walnuts to give to Mum alone
Christmas cheer just wafting throughout our little home
Friends do come a-knocking to wish us happy day
Home's now full of people sitting down to stay
Mum gives out hot toddy, Dad takes up his place
We raise our glasses upward whilst staring at his face
A toast to bless our fortunes, his solemn voice does say
Peace on earth, goodwill to men, to all on Christmas Day.

Lesley Stockley

THE GIFT OF LIFE

Christmas approaches, a time of giving,
But think of the gifts bestowed for living.
Touch and taste and sight and hearing,
Pleasant scents when we are nearing
Flowers and countless other things.
To each of us our Maker brings
Sun and rain and air and light,
All that makes up day and night.
Things we seldom give a thought to,
Yet are gifts we really ought to
Give grateful thanks for every day.
The gift of life alone is marvellous,
But Jesus did even more for us,
He gave His life that we might live
Forever with Him if we believe,
The greatest gift we'll ever receive.

P W Sansom

WISER OR OLDER

As a youth, I waited patiently
For winter to show her face;
When snow fell, it was a joyful event
And to greet it I would race.
Well wrapped in coat, hat, scarf and gloves,
Wellington-clad, I would run
To climb the Welsh mountain, pulling my sledge,
And helter-skelter for fun.

Rosy-cheeked and breathless,
I would scramble
To the very top again,
And hurtle once more,
With many others,
Until the daylight would wane.
Then I would plod reluctantly homewards,
Across fields and through the lanes.

How different my anticipation
Of winter coming today:
Her icy fingers and frozen clutches
Frighten me in every way.
Picturesque blankets of snow are lovely,
But now on postcards only;
Frosted breaths and slippery surfaces
I have no desire to see;
Walking with the melting slush on my legs
Holds no attraction for me.

No more do I look forward to winter's
Coming and getting colder:
Could it be that I have become wiser?
Or have I just grown older?

Terry Daley

HAPPY CHRISTMAS...

When we are young, what does Christmas mean?
Starry-eyed children, who magic have seen,
Santa is magic and turns into mist.
He has to, as chimneys don't always exist.

When we're at school, Nativity plays,
We learn about Jesus and His holy ways.
We're a little confused and a little uptight
But again it's the magic, that makes it alright.

Then there's the bright lights, and Christmas trees,
And Christmas parties with games that do please.
There's turkeys and presents, and Christmas pud,
In all when you're young, Christmas is good...

When we are old, what does Christmas mean?
An expensive time, when things are lean.
We think of all the Christmases past,
And wonder if this one will be our last.
We turn to religion and think about birth
And about Jesus being born on this earth.
Plus what a mess this world is in,
with selfishness, fighting and cruel sin.
We think of loved ones living and dead,
Memories sometimes cause tears to be shed.

But as Christmas is meant to bring us good cheer,
Cheer up
We hope that things will be better next year...

Flora Passant

CHRISTMAS PAST

Scrooge has retreated through a Dickensian door
Burnt candlelight dims on dark ceilings and floors
The church has proclaimed the joy of His birth
Deaf ears are blocked up like dense snow on the earth.

> Cinderella waltzes at her first golden ball
> Whilst credit cards cry through a hole in the wall
> The gifts have been opened; the arguments cease
> With false expectations of love, joy and peace.

Christmas tree lights slowly pop in the dark
Extinguished by hate as the angels sing 'Hark'!
Santas retreat in red cloaks stained with soot
As bitter winds bite with thick frost underfoot.

> Bells have resounded to that first silent night
> Sad, plangent tones echo Man's helpless plight
> Murky mists murder the truth of the Gift
> Like Scrooges all trapped in the icy snowdrift.

Balloons have all burst for the dream is concealed
But who knows - next year - it will all be revealed?
Prickly pine-needles stick to the floor
As Scrooge cries, 'Bah, humbug' from a Dickensian door.

Judy Studd

CHRISTMAS IN THE COUNTRY

Pine trees along the silky roads,
Snow falling everywhere it seems
Makes the country beautiful,
A world of Christmas dreams.

The stars shine down in mystery,
It is the birthday of a King,
I listen to the quiet now
And think I hear the angels sing.

We're coming to the country church,
We'll soon be there to see
The people celebrating joy
Around a Christmas tree.

I'll always love the country where
I've grown to be a part
Of Christmases that last always
Like love inside the heart!

Marion Schoeberlein

I REMEMBER CHRISTMAS

When I think of Christmas,
It reminds me of Jesus' birth
When I think of the Millennium
It reminds me of two thousand years since He came.

When I think of Calvary
It reminds me of the cross
Where the Christ who came was brutally slain.

When I think of God, and His love for mankind
It reminds me of Jesus, whom He sent as a gift
In the form of a baby, born in a lowly stable.

Christmas is a time to reflect on
The mystery of the virgin's birth
And the miracle of the cross
That brings us hope
And the gift of love only God could give.

Joyce A W Edwards-Arnold

SHINE A LIGHT

The spirit of Christmas is with us once more
The season of joy and goodwill,
A time to rejoice and be merry,
With good friends, and glasses to fill.
The wonder on faces of children,
In the morning, when Santa has been,
The smell of mince pies and the pudding
With lashings of brandy and cream!
But let's not forget the true meaning
As we tuck into our turkey and pud,
That a baby was born on this frosty morn,
To show us the meaning of good.
Have a thought for your brethren this Yuletide,
As the good Lord meant it to be,
Shine a light from your heart
And play the right part,
So that God in His Heaven can see.
Then we all can rejoice
And speak with one voice,
When a light down on earth spreads its rays.
Sorrow will cease, and we all can find peace,
To last us the rest of our days.

Linda Storer Smith

Jesus, The Gift Of God

In David's town of Bethlehem
A Saviour had been born
The good news angels joyfully told
Early on Christmas morn
The throngs of angels winged their flight
To tell the world His birth
Proclaiming Him the Wonder God
A Monarch born on earth.

His Name shall be the Prince of Peace
Jesus the Holy Child
The Son of God born of Mary
The blesséd Mother mild,
Jesus the Saviour of the world
God's precious gift to all
Was born in lowliness on earth
Inside a cattle stall.

Jesus the first born Son of God
Pure and divinely bright
was born to lead the human race
In everlasting light
God's promised Word had been fulfill'd
On the birth of His Son
A Child is born, a Son is given
For all the years to come.

Muriel H Beck

You Were The One Love That Would Last: Sadness Is Just A Memory

Don't ask me the reason why
Because I cannot tell you why
Love sometimes makes me cry
It's just that being with you
The whole time through
Makes me feel so happy and sentimental too.

For the sharing is the loving
And through the night our love lasts all the while
The knowing of your beauty the reflection of your smile
Is all I ever wish for all I ever want to know.

Those cold grey days when I was all alone
Mists of time covering the emptiness of my breaking heart
Days and nights of loneliness with sunlight never breaking through
Are now just a sad memory that only now I can begin to bear
For now that I've found complete love with you
I know you will always care.

You were the one love that would last
Amongst all those that time has now passed
I didn't know at first glance
That your sweet love would leave me
In such a permanent trance.

So never let me ache with such sadness again
That bittersweet time with late spring rain
Pouring down like needles of ice so cold
That chilled my heart as the bell tolled.

Never knowing if you had known of my constant love
As it was when nothing could shatter our feelings from above
Don't let the mirror break into fragments of a broken heart
Broken forever so that no one would know of your part.
We played the game and took our chances just like true love romances.

John Docherty

CHRISTMAS EVE

On Christmas Eve
the stars so bright,
Pine trees lit
with glorious light,
Children asleep
their eyes shut tight,
For Father Christmas
descends this night.

Morning the children's eyes
like stars so bright,
Their faces like pine trees
lit with glorious light,
For Father Christmas
has been in the night,
When all little children
slept with eyes shut tight.

Denyce Alexander

BELIEVE

'I don't believe in Father Christmas' she said as she looked at me.
She tugged my beard and snatched my hat as she sat upon my knee.
She screamed aloud as both my hat and beard lay on the floor,
Then broken-hearted leapt from my lap and ran out of the store.
I stood up, my head held low avoiding every stare,
What a fool I felt in my tunic red and my face all flushed and bare.
I walked away, I felt so sad, unwanted and dejected,
A shadowed Santa unveiled to all, no longer now respected.
I lost my job as 'Seasonal Head' but it made me pause and think
Of children disillusioned who have lost their precious link.

Dear parents of all children, I have something to convey,
Please don't lose sight of what it means, our Holy Christmas Day.
We've strayed to times so full of glamour and so full of glitter,
With much induced discontent, which can make joy turn bitter.
We ask for and expect so much, we buy just to receive.
We never ever think of giving because we do believe.
The magic of real Christmas lies not in just red suits,
Or long white curly beards and shiny big black boots,
The dazzle of the lighted trees, the decored splendoured cheer,
It lies within the 'Spirit' that's reborn this time of year.

The next time that your child has doubts about Santa being real,
Remind them of the 'Love' that counts not what beards reveal.
When Heart and Spirit crowns the mind, then don the jolly clothes,
And hand out 'Blessings' with your gifts, then Santa 'Lives' and grows.

Graham Jenkins

CHRISTMAS ROSE

'Daddy, is there really a Father Christmas?
The boys at school, they laugh and joke
Mummies take them to shop for toys
I see lots of people and hear lots of noise.'

My child . . . your children
How many parents face the same dilemma?
Commercialism creates the nothingness
The *Antichrist* within 'The Never-Ending Story'.

'Tiana, do you believe in Daddy Christmas?
Is yours large, cherry-nosed, with a beard?
Sleigh bells, are they in your head?
Do you feel sick with excitement?'

'My daddy's good, he can see what I see
He feels what I feel
Time to cuddle my pillow and fly
Through the clouds . . . with Rudolph high.'

God bless daughter.
Smile in sleep and I will keep
The goblins of commercialism at bay
The lust for money away.

Fly like a fairy upon a breeze
Dream of Christmas, fairies and all
Take your very essence past boundaries
To the foundries of 'The Never-Ending Story'.

The window I place ajar
Carrot, milk and biscuit, setting the scene
I cry a tear with your innocence
Let Christmas be your dream . . .

Andy Rosser

CHRISTMAS GREET

If, on a winter's night, a traveller
should cross the fields of powdered snow,
his cheeks as red as the shining berries
of the sprig of holly in his hand,
should hear the faint white voices
of a hundred children serenading night
and glimpse their bright red lantern's glow,
should feel the warmth of open fires
in houses glittering with tinsel and pine
and humming with expectant hearts,
should note, when passing, your face and mine
so close our breaths embrace, excitement
firing the centres of our desires,
then if, I say, if he should see all this
and murmur still, 'It must be Christmas,'
that then would be self-evident as
if I should say to you
'I love you'.

Howard Young

THE TRUE MESSAGE OF CHRISTMAS

The grey cloak of gloom has descended upon me
At the sight of the first Christmas tree.
It's only November, it's misty and chill,
I do not feel full of unseasonal goodwill.

Christmas is thrust upon us far too soon
To enable the manufacturers to have a boom.
'You must buy this, and you must buy that',
It's so easy to be seduced by the consumer trap.

It's too frantic, too hectic and my head's in a spin,
I'm juggling the money and I just can't win.
Why must we shop as if we're creating a dearth,
Have we forgotten that the true message of Christmas
                                    is 'Peace on Earth'?

Jane Marshall

CHRISTMAS BOX

Christmas - the time to make amends,
Forgive our foes - remember friends,
To share ourselves and share our pleasure
And milk each drop of joy from leisure.
why must this willing, happy, giving,
The living love and loving living,
Hide its glow at other times
In a box with tinsel and angel chimes?

Kate Kerrigan

CHRISTMAS

People shopping like mad at store
I wonder if they remember what Christmas is for?
They push and shove as they go around
Until a bargain can be found.

So much food wasted on the day
I wonder what the homeless would say?
The drink piles up for a few 'boozy' days
Do they think of Jesus born on this earth?
Oh, what a glorious birth.

If only this earth was how it should be
Without any pain
Where we had got
Everything to gain.

Sinners we all are
But we can all try to change
To have peace on this earth would take a lot
But never let Jesus be forgot.

Trisha Moreton

A Christmas Wish

They helped her onto Santa's knee
  Lights twinkled on a tinselled tree
    A pretty girl with auburn hair
      Santa held her with such tender care

        Have you a special wish?
          Have you brought me a list?
            Do you want a new computer?
              What present can I bring you?

                The girl gave Santa her shy look
                  Please don't bring me games or books
                  Computers, clothes or any toys
                Keep those for other girls and boys

                My wish for Xmas is so very small
                To be completely normal, that is all
                  Please make my legs grow straight and strong
                How can this Xmas wish be wrong?

                  They helped her from his red-clad knee
                  He turned his head so she could not see
                  The sad tears that pricked his eyes
                  A child should not see a grown man cry.

Jane Manning

YULETIDE

Celebration, coming together,
making every Christmas
a memory forever.

Little fingers tearing pretty paper,
and bows and ribbons,
a time for giving.
A new year, a time for a change.

Away in a manger,
mince pies and hot tea.
Every Christmas has a special
but different meaning to me.

L J Needs

WHAT'S LEFT AFTER CHRISTMAS?

What have we left now that Christmas has gone?
The parties are over, we had *so* much fun
Bottles are empty - food gone to waste
Folk milling around - sad looks on their face
Toys are now broken - cast in the bin
They cost so much money - it seems such a sin
Presents discarded - clothes we'll not wear
What's left after Christmas? Utter despair.

The tree and trimmings are all stripped bare
Stored in the loft - awaiting next year
The debts are piled high - maybe twelve months to pay
Then we'll be round to a new Christmas Day
The spirit of Christmas - seemed everyone had
Has vanished so quickly - how terribly sad
Why is it they're empty - searching in vain?
What's left after Christmas? Misery and pain.

Many people are treading the road of despair
So let us tell of Jesus and show that we care
Point to the road - the only true way
To the foot of the cross - do not delay
Then Christmas will mean so much to their heart
For Christ who is in it will never depart
He'll be with them forever - in eternity too
What's left after Christmas?
                God's love - pure and true.

B M Howard

THE MESSAGE

Christmas time - once again,
That time of good cheer,
When candle-lights shadows,
Bid farewell, to another year.

Snowflakes dance,
To the peal of church bells,
As carol singers' voices, echo
The final noels.

Thoughts and good wishes,
- Of a peaceful world -
At a time of remembering,
- The Saviour's birth.

- Truly blessed -
The meek and the mild,
Wide open eyes, sparkling
In every young child.

Hope for the future,
In the knowledge and belief,
That from a manger, within a lowly stable,
Arose - the uncrowned Prince of Peace.

Born - of love and caring,
A Father's one and only Son,
Who was to make the ultimate sacrifice,
- To give His life -
That others might live on.

Bakewell Burt

CHRISTMAS TIME 1999

Downtown shoppers rushing to and fro
Carrying traditional wrapping paper
Presents and mistletoe
Children gaze with starry eyes
At twinkling decorations
Hoping Santa Claus
Will be bringing a surprise
Everywhere there's a festive scene
Beautiful wreaths, delightful poinsettia
Of seasonal red and green
There's a choir singing carols
Around the tall decorated tree
Shoppers linger and join them
Forgetting all their urgency
Long queues at the checkout tills
People meeting old friends
Wish each other goodwill
Every town and village
Becomes a fairylight wonderland
I hope all children
Remember and understand
Whilst they unwrap their presents
This special Christmas morn
      2000 years ago
Our Lord and Saviour
Jesus Christ was born
And as church bells ring
To celebrate the Saviour's birth
Let hearts hope and pray
For peace upon this earth.

Joan Taylor

CHRISTMAS

Christmas is such a wonderful time,
buying gifts for families and friends.
Decorations, trees and sparkling lights,
But how many of us think of the message this sends?

We're celebrating the birth of Jesus,
who was born on the 25th of December.
He came into the world to save you and I,
Therefore, Jesus we should always remember.

so as you give out your Christmas gifts,
and sit down to your Christmas meal,
Think of Jesus whose birthday it is,
and feel your love for Him is real.

Carole Osselton

WAR CHILD

No Christmas treats in store for those
no greatest story ever told
no fairy lights or mistletoe
no flying reindeer to behold

No jingle bells or silent night
no roast chestnuts or hot mince pies
no presents opened with delight
no wide excited eyes

For me this day is like any other
away from my friends, my father, my mother
the Holy Infant was tender and mild
so spare a thought for the war child.

Wayne Cregan

Nobody Cares
(For Joany)

You sit there alone in your worn old armchair,
A sad-eyed old lady with silvery hair.
No-one could tell you how long you've been there,
For nobody knows you,
And nobody cares.
You think of the past, and the times you have cried,
Through the long lonely hours by your cold fireside.
You live in a dream-world that nobody shares,
For nobody needs you,
And nobody cares.
.Remember your friends, and the way they would laugh,
Now all you have left is an old photograph;
A tattered reminder of happier years,
But nobody knows them,
And nobody cares.
Time eats away at the pittance you saved,
And the young man you married is ten years in his grave.
You listen each night for his tread on the stairs,
But nobody hears him,
And nobody cares.
But as your eyes close for the very last time,
Leaving the world that forgot you behind,
You'll smile for the first time in many a year,
And no-one will notice,
And no-one will care.

Kevin J Hodge

KOSOVO CHILD

You are the Kosovo child
born to be free, born to be wild

Yet through your eyes I see genocide that now makes you feel pain
inflicted by those who have nothing to gain

looking through the Kosovo child's eyes
seeing death all around and hearing the Kosovo people's cries

Yes Kosovo child you will shed many tears
over and over and over the years
but time will heal to allay your fears

I know that you often pray
that your nightmares will just go away
do not worry you will live a new day

You will live with the genocide you have witnessed every day
yet time will heal your wounds and your memories will gradually fade
away
so go now Kosovo child and play

Wally

A Time To Remember

As we celebrate Christmas and have a good feed,
Let us try to remember, those people in need.
In war-torn countries, living in tents,
Let them hear our prayers, from heaven sent.

The festive spirit, all merry and bright,
Just spare a thought for the homeless and not forget their plight.
While we are enjoying ourselves and having a good time,
There are plenty less fortunate, who haven't got a dime.

Before we sit down to eat our Christmas fayre,
Let us all pray together, to show them we care.
The needy, the homeless and those all alone,
Who haven't got anyone, not even a phone.

G Silver

A Christmas Thought

When comes this time of happiness
brings with it all its sadness
what's already been, and yet to come
we remember, waiting to see,
we love and love being loved,
searching the true meaning of Christmas
Nativity at its finest
as the children sing in chorus
choirs ring out silent night
emotional time we think of others,
together thoughts of our own anguish
a time of year that brings about,
the closeness of families
festivities, gifts and good food
as we remember those less fortunate
may it snow on this Christmas Day.

Sharon Evans

The Hotel

That was David's name for it,
We seemed to be there forever.
We escaped every day
And walked in the world together.
He was a modern Shakespearean drama teacher,
I was a run down Mum just resting,
The time we stayed at the hotel place
We helped each other by sharing.
His world had crashed about him,
His job, his marriage gone.
My life was shattered and torn.
Night was here. The sun no longer shone.
We left that place and went our separate ways
We bid goodbye, we'd seen that side of life and shared it.
I wonder to this day if David made it.

Joan E Blissett

CELEBRATING CHRISTMAS

I can see a wonderful star above,
Such a crisp night . . .
For there is no roof above my head,
Bare earth the bed from which I view.
In happier times we sang of a leading star:
A Babe born humbly in a simple stable.
My neighbour bore a child last night,
Her birth pangs staining where she lay -
The only memory of the two.
This morning they were carried together,
To the lime pit.
The feasts we had! - The thoughts cramp my stomach now.
My tongue tore when I licked my tin
To catch the last drop of - whatever it was,
Bile rises at the possibilities.
The Holy Babe fled from His homeland;
Little Lordling, now I understand.
Look down. Pity us.
I can feel Your tears in the dew,
It was not for this You died.
The star seems to be brighter
As if the rays would form a path.
Is this Your Christmas gift to me,
To share Your natal feast with You?

Dear Friend, I come . . .

Di Bagshawe

CHRISTMAS SPIRIT?

Christmas time is here again
Bringing joy – or is it pain?
First there's all the frantic shopping,
Then the sound of corks a-popping.
Same old story every year:
Too much 'champers', too much beer.
We rush about from shop to shop
Until we're nearly fit to drop.
Have we bought enough to eat?
We've got the veg and got the meat.
We've made the cake and made the pud,
We've got the turkey – oh, that's good.
On we go then – huffing, puffing –
Mind we don't forget the stuffing!
We spend and spend – we feel we must –
And eat until we're fit to bust!
We drink too much and never doubt
That this is what it's all about.
The trouble is there's too much greed,
We eat and drink more than we need.
If only we would stop and think
(Between the food, between the drink)
Of others far less fortunate,
With empty cup and empty plate,
Who at Christmas cannot cope,
Who have no home and have no hope.
Please let us all love one another,
Instead of self, think of each other.
And then perhaps the greed would cease
And we would all find Christmas peace.

Anne Brown

WINTER THOUGHTS

Crisp cold hardens the earth.
We cut away dead growth,
clear away the debris,
neaten beds, sweep wet leaves.
All living things must rest;
sleep before rejuvenation.

Indoors most humans bask in central heating.
Glad we are what we are,
frail to winter's worst,
protected by modern technology.

But not the homeless.
Newspaper wrapped, boxed by cardboard,
they suffer hypothermia,
lack of food, bleeding chilblains:
a torture from the past.

They are not dead growth
to be swept away as debris.
They need nurturing before rejuvenation.

Christmas can only be enjoyed from safety.
When experience of the elements
is crowned by the refuge of home.

Gwen Hartland

A Moral Millennium

Another thousand years have gone
While man's search for knowledge remains,
The outer planets which have shone
Are the next for conquest and gains.
Great minds have left us joy and wealth,
Their genius there for all to see,
But talent does not bring good health
With all the plagues of history.
With celebrations at their height,
We should divert our inward stare
And look to children and their plight,
Then offer what we have, to share.
Each little face which feels the cold
As parents rot beneath the sky,
Needs someone's hand to touch and hold,
They should be told the reasons why.
We take enormous steps to see
The future shining ever bright,
And yet we fail humanity
As warring factions kill and fight.
Our conscience does not run too deep,
For each night when we close the door,
We turn out backs on those who weep
Amid the poverty and gore.
So as the fireworks pierce the sky
And minds are warped by flowing wine,
Just watch the smoke that's drifting by,
A young girl may have tripped a mine.
Another thousand years have fled,
We must enjoy ourselves this year,
Let's taste the wine and break the bread,
We scream with joy, but others fear.

Doug Thomas

POPPIES OF FLANDERS' FIELDS

In pride old soldier marches to Cenotaph on Remembrance Day, medals, colour ribbons fall over his heart of 104 years. One single poppy in beret, he kneels before Cenotaph, there his poppy wreath he lay. Young voices question why the poppy and not the rose or maybe violets blue. Old soldier salutes Cenotaph, four steps back, slow march, he links with voice of question, reply with words true. The battlefields of France, Flanders and Picardy, most bloodbaths world have ever known, so much loss of blood as red river begins to flow. Dark shadows murmur and veil the sky awaiting the time of deaths to mourn. Young soldiers in mud and mire trenches close their eyes ready to meet their fates. Each soldier a poem to love. One did write in a world of love and hate, there is no sterner sorrow than that of a soldier to have for his mate. Lone trumpeter calls *Last Post* for souls who from heaven cry, if to play *Last Post* for every valiant heart who for peace his life he give then for another 500 years the lonesome call would echo through the sky. In Flanders' fields dead heroes lie, millions of white crosses row on row. Wings of wind whisper watch over peaceful fields of white no more to be the dark of night. Where once river of blood did flow millions of red poppies in their glory grow and from a distance resemble a river of blood, a vision of sight to know. Poets rest neath wings of wind and why the world wants to know where was God in this nightmare inferno battle leaving us with a poppy for every valiant heart and millions of white crosses row on row.

Phyllis Blue

WAR YEARS 1914 TO 1918

I remember when I was very young my dad went to war in
                                          World War One.
He was sent to France to fight, leaving behind his wife, two
                                          daughters and a son.
Those days were very dreary, no electricity just candles and an oil
                                          lamp to give us light,
No wireless or television to let us know what the future had in sight.
I can picture my dad now when he used to come home on leave,
Polishing all his buttons on a gadget he put on his sleeve.
Rolling up his putties round his trousers and up his legs
Making them look just like a couple of pegs.
One day my mum had a telegram to say he was missing presumed dead,
It was a terrible shock to us, the suspense we did dread,
Till we heard the news he was the only one saved out of his lot,
His Guardian Angel was with him and a great hand from God.
As the years went by and peace was with us once more
We could go out in peace and do the things we did adore.
I remember the high top boots my dad bought for my sister and me,
We had to lace them up so high almost to our knee.
Then he bought mum a piano it was their pride and joy,
It was a luxury those days and did those ivory keys ring, 'Oh Boy'.
It gave us so much pleasure and helped us to forget the war years
                                                                     we had
And that God saved our dad and we were all glad.

Olive Peck

A Christmas Wish

Time now to start dreaming,
The clouds are hanging low,
Covering the hilltops,
That are all white with snow.

Magic sledge will take you,
So warm and safe inside,
To Bethlehem and back,
Get ready for the ride.

Christmas fairies feed you,
With fine delicious things,
All the way to Dreamland,
With sleep dust on their wings.

Northern Lights are shining,
By twinkling stars lit bright,
Look for a better world,
Beyond this holy night.

Christ child too was homeless,
He knows what makes you cry,
Sends love down to find you,
From heaven in the sky.

Christmas angels bring you,
Much better future days,
For you are so precious,
They think of you always.

Be kind to each other,
You're lucky to have friends,
Sharing on the journey,
To love that never ends.

Kathleen Mary Scatchard

SPARE A THOUGHT AT CHRISTMAS

I feel sorry for the people who are poor,
Standing there lonely, looking at your door,
So, please let them in,
Because they just can't win,
All they want to do -
Is spend Christmas with someone like you,
That's why I -
Feel sorry for the people who are poor.

Janine Thomas (10)

A Prayer

Dear Lord.

We pray for those children
Who are lost and alone
In the world:

Who have no mother
To keep them safe
From the evils of life;
To tuck them up in bed at night;
To hug them and wish them sweet dreams.

Whose father they've lost
In the battles of war,
With only photographs
Of their memory,
Wrapped in brown paper,
Tattered and torn.

And the children who go hungry
In these times of plenty,
Begging on street corners
For scraps of meat,
Scratching around in the dirt
For grains of corn
Dropped from sacks
Of passers-by.

And Lord
At this special time of year,
Show them the love as you did your son,
Welcome them into your heart
As we welcomed your son:
Jesus Christ Our Saviour.

Amen.

Marcus Tyler

GIVE US HOPE

Give us hope oh Lord please do
We need your courage to see us through
Give us hope oh Lord we cry
Show us your kindness or we may die

Give us hope oh Lord we pray
So that we may see another day
Give us hope oh Lord my friend
We will love you till the end

Give us hope oh Lord, we thirst
For a sign that we come first
.Give us hope oh Lord be praised
We'll worship you Lord for all our days

Valerie Deering

NO ONE CARES

The holly, the berries, the Christmas cheer
Go down well with a couple of beers
But remember the people that have none
And you can bet your life it's no fun
Sleeping on a cold paving slab
And their feet have split through the sleeping bag
The ice is pinching their toes
Just give a thought to all their woes
They didn't ask to be on the street
They would like a soft bed
And a roof over their head
But all they've got is a pavement instead
Bad luck has followed them down the spiral stairs
And all people that walk by just give a stare
A merry Christmas is what they would like
But the people just say get on your bike
Maybe they will get help one day
But the government just tell them to go away.

Joy Willoughby

Just A Glimmer

Oh spirit of light enter into this new Millennium
Shine in its' corners where there is darkness
Enter the deep troubles of peoples' minds
Setting them free from fear, violence and terror.

May sunbeams dance with joy and gladness
Like rays of jewels resting on a silent breath
Bringing some light onto an arid desert
Where life seems suppressed and nothing grows.

Beam onto countries bringing security and hope
Into ravaged children who see parents taken away
Crying for someone to stop this hurt inside
One caring person to hold them, to cuddle them.

May their faces shine with a new confidence
Entering into a new century with faithful hearts
Growing up in a world that wants peace.
So all people work together side by side.

Bringing the light of Jesus as a lamp unto their feet
Going before them step by step guiding the way
Until they realise there can be a bright future.
Just a glimmer turns to radiant light.

Margaret Davies

CHRISTMAS LOVE

Christmas comes with celebrations once a year
Bringing along blessings of good hope and cheer,
Our thoughts travel back in time to a Baby dear
Who was born to be mankind's promised Saviour.

Christmas is a time to recall all our friends,
Truly forgive and make amends,
To review our actions as the old year ends,
Make fresh resolutions while the new descends.

Christmas is a happy time for most of us,
Loving thoughts and gifts we exchange between us.
But we are more blest when we do realise
That others less fortunate are in need of us.

Christmas is the time to start to care,
With the destitute our bread and salt to share.
To give to the old, sick and those in despair
A helping hand for their cross to bear.

For the lonely also a thought we must spare
Be it an old man or a maiden fair.
Love is needed all year round and everywhere,
To forget that we must never, never dare.

Christmas is the time to show true love
To a fellow-human or a dog or dove.
Love is a gift sent from heaven above
For love is God and God is love.

Alice Zamanian

SPARE A THOUGHT

We are from a poor family
War has taken its toll
Spare a thought for all of us
We are hungry and cold.
Christmas should be a joyful time
Spare a thought and share
We don't mind what it is
We know you really care.
A Christmas tree we do not have
Or tinsel around the house
But spare a thought for us
A toy and food will do
When we get these gifts
We will be thinking of you too.

Pauline M Wardle

JESUS HOLD MY HAND

Oh Jesus, are you there
Take away these doubts and show us that you care
Can't you see, your children's fear
Comfort us and show us you are near

Take us by the hand and lead us safely through the valley
Where the devil lurks and tempts us to cast off each load we carry
To take the easy way and care not for our fellow man
Oh Jesus, oh Jesus, Jesus take us by the hand

Is it right that we should work to get what others get for nothing
Are the pleasures of the flesh worth more than deep sincere loving
Are the famines and the tempest all part of your master plan
Oh Jesus, oh Jesus, Jesus take us by the hand

You taught us to give only love and turn the other cheek
If we want to be taken to the heaven that we seek
But temptation stalks the road we tread to reach that promised land
Oh Jesus, oh Jesus, Jesus take us by the hand

Don Woods

SPARE A THOUGHT

Spare a thought for people with nowhere to live,
Spare a thought for people with nothing to give,
Spare a thought for people living on the street,
Spare a thought for people with nothing to eat.

Spare a thought for people who are ill,
Spare a thought you can take a pill,
Spare a thought for people who are dying,
Spare a thought for people who are crying,
Spare a thought this Christmas time,
Being homeless is their only crime.

Kane Saunders (11)

Just Spare A Thought

Yuletide is here again,
For many a time of good cheer
Backslapping and hearty congratulations
Heady wine and frothy beer . . .
But for many it brings loneliness,
Heartbreak and no cheer,
A time of trepidation,
Uncertainty and fear:
Remember too a child was born
In a stable rude and bare,
Poverty was His mantle,
Everlasting love His fare . . .
And as festive joys surround you
Remember what He taught:
Always consider others and their needs . . .
Just spare a thought.

Arthur Pickles

A Child's Cry For Peace

I look at my home, a war-torn city
From the rest of the world a feeling of pity
This was a people of sweetness and cheer
But, all this has been replaced by continual fear.

Who fired the first shot into this town?
Who shot the mortars, and, brought the spirits down?
Who wins the battle when the day is done?
The answer is simply, no one.

The power and the glory, eternal man's greed
To win another's country, they don't actually need.
The mind or the spirit, to what do they listen
Where is their conscience when into battle they hasten.

Who feeds the hungry, who buries the dead?
How many families broken, how many fled?
Material or spiritual, what offers the most
To live a good life or, to race for the post.

To war all things are changed for the worst
Nothing is gained, everyone's hurt
Make the most of the peace, do what you can
Tomorrow could be war, and your worst enemy's man.

Lynda Fordham

SPARE A THOUGHT

Spare a thought
Just one moment only,
for those bereaved, and sick, the poor,
and lonely,
This Christmas time.
Think of those
imprisoned by some cruel nation,
As you deck the holly,
and pin up that decoration,
This Christmas time.
Pray for those people
who face a firing squad,
As you sing you carol,
and worship God,
This Christmas time.
Peace on Earth
is our Saviour's plan.
Why then, do we mistreat
our fellowman?
This Christmas time.
Because he's coloured,
or lame, and less able,
Is this why Jesus
was born in a stable?
This Christmas time.

Gordon Bannister

REMEMBER THEM

There are many this Christmastide
Who are homeless and alone.
They are victims of oppression
And have nothing of their own.
There are no friends around them
No bright lit Yuletide tree.
Look down O Lord and bless them
Wherever they may be.

Remember too the children
Who will have no toys.
They will hear no sleigh bells
'Nor have no Christmas joys.
Let us pray to God the Father
For the sake of His dear son
To remember those in desolation
And bless them everyone.

Mary Ferguson

SPARE JUST ONE MINUTE

Think of Christmas,
While all the poor
Gather around the kitchen door,
Hoping for food,
Have you got a little to spare?
Showing these people you really care.

Tara Woods (10)

SPARE A THOUGHT

Spare a thought for the poor,
Don't be greedy and just take,
Remember to also give,
While we are all eating delicious turkey
They are wondering where their next meal is coming from,
So spare a thought for the poor.

Dean Hallett (10)

WHAT HARM COULD IT DO TO HELP A POOR PERSON?

Just spare a thought for poor children
Wandering on the streets.
Just think of yourself
Eating lots of sweets.
But they do not have a choice
About their miserable day.
Missing out on Christmas
While they sit and pray.

Jemma Hall (10)

SPARE A THOUGHT

Spare a thought for the ones in need,
Spare a thought when your cards you read,
Spare a thought when you decorate your tree,
Spare a thought when your presents you see.

Spare a thought for the homeless and the poor,
Spare a thought when you ask for more,
Spare a thought for the people who are dying,
Spare a thought for those who are always crying.

Spare a thought for the people on the street,
Spare a thought when you sit down to eat,
Spare a thought - make the people aware,
Spare a thought - show that you care.

Matthew Reeves (10)

THINK OF OTHERS

Can you spare a single minute
To think of those who are just not with it,
While you're playing with lots of toys,
Think of other girls and boys,
When you're sitting on the floor,
Think of those who are really poor,
While you're sitting in a nice warm bath,
Think of those who need a laugh,
So spare a thought and think of others,
Maybe with your sisters and brothers.

Kayleigh Gosling (10)

SPIRIT OF CHRISTMAS

People forget
The spirit of Christmas
While they are having
So much fun,
People forget why
Christmas is really here,
You shouldn't forget that
It is Jesus' birthday
And that you should be thankful
That all your family is near.

Laura Carpenter (10)

SPARE A THOUGHT

Just think carefully when you're having
Such fun at Christmas time,
Of the people in Palestine,
How poor they are,
They don't even get a chocolate bar.
When you're partying at night,
Poor children have nobody to love or fight,
So please spare a thought,
For all the lonely, poor people.

Jessica Twydall (10)

SPARE A THOUGHT

Spare a thought for those in need,
Who are homeless, yes indeed,
Who beg by day,
Who beg by night,
Help them in their desperate plight,
So please while you are on your way
Spare a thought on Christmas Day.

Kayleigh Stannage (11)

SPARE A THOUGHT

Spare a thought
for other people,
Not rich nor famous
but poor and feeble.
They search for water
everyday,
They try to find it
in any way.
Just spare a thought
for other people,
Give them something for
Christmas,
Just one small little thing
would cheer them up.
So spare a thought
for other people.

Gina Curtis (11)

SPARE A THOUGHT

Spare a thought for the poor,
Don't be greedy,
Just remember we've got more
Than those who are hungry and locked out,
We should remember - not forget
That they are poor,
Just spare a thought.

Alex Payne (10)

CHRISTMAS

The festive season, when the cold winds blow,
Brings us good cheer, which makes our hearts glow;
Brings us warm thoughts of the ones we hold dear,
And our hearts rejoice, for Christmas is here.

A time for the holly and mistletoe,
For the bright lights and soft candleglow;
A time for the tree, with gifts to adorn,
For the laughter of children on Christmas morn.

Amidst all this wonder, let us not cease,
To think of our Lord, who came to bring peace;
To think of that night in Bethlehem,
When a child was born, the Saviour of men.

A tiny babe, in a stable lowly,
Just a humble place, yet made so holy;
By the presence of God in human form,
By the presence of love which makes a home.

May love and joy in all our homes abide,
May happiness be ours this Christmastide;
May the nations rejoice, the whole world sing,
Praises to our Millennium King.

Brenda Radford

INFORMATION

We hope you have enjoyed reading this book - and that you will continue to enjoy it in the coming years.

If you like reading and writing poetry drop us a line, or give us a call, and we'll send you a free information pack.

Write to :-
**Triumph House Information
Remus House
Coltsfoot Drive
Woodston
Peterborough
PE2 9JX
(01733) 898102**